room 1

Garden Suburb Junior School
Childs Way
London NW11 6XU
Tel: 020 8455 3269
Fax: 020 8457 5199

The Magic Box

Also published by Macmillan Children's Books

I Had a Little Cat
Collected Poems for Children
Charles Causley

Sensational!
Poems inspired by the five senses
Chosen by Roger McGough

The Jumble Book
Poems chosen by Roger Stevens

KIT WRIGHT

The Magic Box

POEMS FOR CHILDREN

Illustrated by Peter Bailey

MACMILLAN CHILDREN'S BOOKS

First published 2009 by Macmillan Children's Books
a division of Macmillan Publishers Limited
20 New Wharf Road, London N1 9RR
Basingstoke and Oxford
Associated companies throughout the world
www.panmacmillan.com

ISBN 978-0-230-70515-9

1 3 5 7 9 8 6 4 2

A CIP catalogue record for this book is available from
the British Library.

Printed and bound in the UK by CPI Mackays, Chatham ME5 8TD

Contents

Introduction

I've gathered together in this book most of the poems I've written for children; that is, nearly everything from the collections *Rabbiting On, Hot Dog* and *Great Snakes*, and a generous helping of the poems in *Cat Among the Pigeons*. I have also included the words of two picture books, *Dragonella* and *Tigerella*.

There are some new, uncollected pieces, including two songs, 'Farmer Jessop' and 'The Thumb Bird', a sort of blues-style rap ('Bad Dog Blues') and one or two poems written specially for this book. I've also included a handful of poems that I wrote for adults (that's my other job) but that children like and that I very often perform in schools. If a few seem just a bit hard to understand fully yet, I hope enough comes through for you to enjoy them now and perhaps get to know them more deeply in time.

There are plenty of serious poems here, both inward-looking and outward-looking, and many whose main ambition is to make you smile or laugh. The title poem, 'The Magic Box', was written a long time ago as a model to help children make their own poems, following the same loose formula. I have seen many thousands of excellent Magic Boxes! And my own poem here is a slight variant on the original, since every time you play this game it turns out differently.

I thought *The Magic Box* would also be a good title for this collection. Let's hope you find something magical in it to enjoy!

Kit Wright

Red Boots On

Way down Geneva,
All along Vine,
Deeper than the snow drift
Love's eyes shine.

Mary Lou's walking
In the winter time.

She's got

Red boots on, she's got
Red boots on,
Kicking up the winter
Till the winter's gone.

So

Go by Ontario,
Look down Main,
If you can't find Mary Lou,
Come back again.

Sweet light burning
In winter's flame.

She's got

Snow in her eyes, got
A tingle in her toes
And new red boots on
Wherever she goes

So

All around Lake Street,
Up by St Paul,
Quicker than the white wind
Love takes all.

Mary Lou's walking
In the big snow fall.

She's got

Red boots on, she's got
Red boots on,
Kicking up the winter
Till the winter's gone.

Loose Cannons and Crazy Characters

Nutter

The moon's a big white football,
The sun's a pound of butter.
The earth is going round the twist
And I'm a little nutter!

Some People

You can't tell some people anything.

I told my friend a secret.
'It dies with me,' he said.
Then he dropped dead.

You can't tell some people anything.

Cheering Up Ivan

When Catherine the Great met Ivan the Terrible
Down at the old Pier Head,

It was, 'How are you, Cath?'
'I'm great! And you?'
'Terrible,' Ivan said.

'Cheer up, son! We'll phone William the Silent.
He'll know what to do.

Bill, is that you?
Bill, is that you?
Bill?'

A Bit of Luck for Sonia

I wish you were sunnier, Sonia,
I wish you'd the happiness knack.
I wish you kept saying, 'Good on yer!'
And giving me pats on the back.

But wishes are wasted upon yer,
For chumminess never you'll learn,
So, Sonia, I'm off to Bologna,
And don't think I'll ever return!

The Chap

I happened once to know a chap:
You may have known him too –

But only, of course, if your chap's name
Was in every way the very same
As the name of the chap I knew.

But if by the merest whisker
Those names are out of line,

Then my chap, poor chap, wasn't your chap,
Your chap wasn't mine!

Doris

There was a young lady called Doris
Who had a twin sister called Chloris,
    One brother called Maurice,
    Another called Norris
And two more called Horace and Boris.

Now Doris was quite fond of Chloris
And she didn't mind Maurice or Norris
    But she hated Horace
    And Horace loathed Boris

And Horace, Boris, Maurice, Norris
and Chloris couldn't take Doris *at
any price at all.*

Fenby

November hung its head in gloom
When Fenby led us to his room.

He sat us down and right away
Announced to all who cared to stay:

'I cannot undertake to state
A single thing. I can't relate

'One episode of all of time.
I cannot fall. I cannot climb.

'I cannot break. I cannot mend.
I can't begin. I cannot end.

'I cannot name the reason why
I cannot live but cannot die.'

'Bad luck!' said someone, maybe me,
And wondered if a cup of tea

Was totally beyond his powers.
'I can't. I cannot count the hours

'I've failed to make the tea-bag swim.
I cannot bring it to the brim.'

At which I heard an oldster call:
'CAN YOU DO ANYTHING AT ALL

'OF ANY USE IN ANY WAY?'
And Fenby said: 'I cannot say.'

Zoe's Ear-rings

She bought 'em in the autumn
After spotting 'em in Nottingham.
She took 'em home to Cookham
And she put 'em in a drawer

Till May came and the day came
When she wore 'em down to Shoreham,
But *nobody* was for 'em
So she wore 'em nevermore . . .

Till the wedding of her sister
To a mister out at Bicester,
Name of Jimmy, who said, '*Gimme*,'
So without 'em she went home,

But she nipped back down to nick 'em
For a knees-up in High Wycombe,
For an evening quite near Chevening
And a dawn at Kilmacolm.

They were in 'er for a dinner
Which was excellent, in Pinner,
And another one, a cracker,
In Majacca – that's in Spain –

Then she popped 'em on in Haddenham
And didn't feel too bad in 'em:
She felt in 'em, in Cheltenham,
Just as right as rain.

They looked smart on in Dumbarton,
They looked wizard on the Lizard,
They looked corking down in Dorking
And incredible in Crewe.

When she wore 'em into Rugely
They impressed the people hugely,
While in Fordham folk adored 'em,
And they *loved* 'em in West Looe!

The citizens of Kettering
Had never seen a better ring,
In fact no better pair of 'em –
'Take care of 'em!' they cried.

Then she slithered into Lytham with 'em,
Shaking out a rhythm with 'em,
Wobb-er-ling and jogg-er-ling
Her head from side to side.

Folk in Preston thought the best 'un
Was the right 'un. In New Brighton
And in Sefton, though, the *left* 'un
Was the one they favoured more,

While in Greenham, when they'd seen 'em,
They said, 'How to choose between 'em?
What one praises in its brother,
In the *other* one is for!'

Then she tried 'em with new make-up
On a sponsored run round Bacup,
And at Norwich for a porridge-
Eating contest which she won,

But, spilling 'em in Gillingham,
Her lobes felt light in Willingham,
And nothing else is filling 'em,
So now

The poem's

Done!

Mariannagram

The happiest discovery
Of all her life and times?
The **MERRY CHRISTMAS** anagram
Of **MR STARRYCHIMES**!

Animal Oddments

The Rabbit's Christmas Carol

I'm sick as a parrot,
I've lost me carrot,
I couldn't care less if it's
Christmas Day.

I'm sick as a parrot,
I've lost me carrot,
So get us a lettuce
Or . . . go away!

The Budgie's New Year Message

Get a little tin of bird-seed,
Pour it in my little trough.
If you don't, you little twit, I'll
Bite your little finger off!

A Little Night Music

I lay awake at midnight
And a smile was on my face
As I heard the caterwauling
Of the cats in Feline Place.
They were bawling, they were yowling,
And they yodelled at the moon.

I grinned a grin: for *my* cat
Was the *only* cat in tune!

I sprang awake at 5 a.m.
The dogs in Canine Square
Were barking out a Bach Chorale
And barking mad they were.
They angered all the neighbourhood
And terrified the birds.

I grinned a grin: for *my* dog,
And *he only*, knew the words!

So

Tickle my funny-bone nightly,
Tickle my funny-bone, do!
You can't get bamboo shoots at Boots
But you can get Boots shampoo –

Oi!

The Tears of Things

When cows are cowed
and sheep
are sheepish

in the deep
they feel it
deepish.

How they mourn
for each
landlubber.

Fish sing scales
of grief.
Whales

blubber.

Incident on the Island

Once upon the Isle of Thanet
I was sitting by the sea
When a gull, or else a gannet,
Landed something on my knee.

By my side my old friend Janet
Loudly laughed at my mishap.
What an island! What a planet!
What a way to treat a chap!

Swaybacks in the Springtime

Two old horses, piebald swaybacks,
Mooching down by the chestnut trees:
Sharing a field in spring, though these
Are the winter days of their lives.

Two old horses, put out to grass here,
Suddenly break, frisk into a run
And their tough manes gleam in the rising sun
In the winter days of their lives.

The Fall of Cleopatra

Three in a tree-house,
tree-house trio,
up in an ash
with a dog named Cleo.

Two were girls
and one was a fella
and the loudest child was
Isabella.

The dog fell off
their sky-borne raft
and Isabella
laughed &
  "   &
  "   &
  "   &
  "   &
  "   &
  "   &
  "   &

felt a bit sick.

In Cold Blood

Some snakes are secrets
that issue themselves from shadows
and spoon their heads onwards to follow
their forking tongues

in a system of S's,
successively slithering silently,
always on oil, and wrapping
their rings round rungs.

They never stop growing
and when they need roomier garments
they wrestle their skins off and dump them
inside out.

They bite their way free
from eggs like spuds or parsnips.
Fangs are a kettle of venom's
double spout.

Some eat each other,
and some will consume a whole leopard,
then fast for a year, while some
can swallow a goat.

Some get a crush
on a creature and squeeze its heart
till it slides down the long canal
like a narrow boat.

None vegetarian,
many are wonderfully beautiful,
jewel-ropes of green
and copper and gold

on tree, grass, rock,
in the sea. They have their sorrows,
and die if they ever eat anything
too cold . . .

The Publishing Puffin

A puffin on her native cliff
Above the breakers foaming white
Spied in the rock a hieroglyph
And read it with immense delight.
Her mind's eye took a photostat.
'I think,' she said, 'I'll publish that.'

And publish it she did indeed,
As also works of guillemots
And terns, and every other breed
Of sea-bird in the coastal spots,
Until word sped of her on land
And human songs she took in hand.

And that is why this very day
Above those crags and hollowed crypts
People queue with things to say,
Authors bearing manuscripts,
Hoping that they might bring joy
To sea-bird, or to girl or boy.

The Very First People on Earth

Did the very first people on earth rejoice
At being the earth's first people?

They did not.

They stood about kicking at lumps of flint
And sneered at their situation.

'Why hasn't Concorde been invented?' they cried.
'Then we could get
The hell out of here.'

And 'You can't even get a cup of tea!' they moaned.
And 'Why is that mammoth mammoth
Glowering from that rock?

'Why is that mammoth mammoth
Glowering from that rock?

'Why is that mammoth ma–'

The Balham Alligator

If you walk up Balham High Road
And you wander down a by-road
To the common and the woods
That lie beyond,

You will meet if you are patient there
An animal that's stationed there,
An alligator living
In the pond . . .

He's the BALHAM ALLIGATOR on the run, run, run,
And he's hiding from his Keeper
In the Zoo!

To the Zoo he took a scunner
Which is why he done a runner
And he's waiting there
Just for
You!

So if you care to stay with him
And pass the time of day with him
And have a heart-to-heart there,
One to one,

(That's if you've got the bottle)
He will like it quite a lottle,
Will the Balham Alligator
On the run!

Oh, the BALHAM ALLIGATOR on the run, run, run,
They took him from the swamp
Across the sea,

And he found his new home horrider
In every way than Florida
And that's how
He comes to
Be . . .
The . . .

BALHAM ALLIGATOR on the run, run, run!
Oh, he's hiding from his Keeper
In the Zoo!

To the Zoo he took a scunner
Which is why he done a runner
And he's waiting there
Just for
You!

Watch out.

Our Hamster's Life

Our hamster's life:
there's not much
to it,
not much
to it.

He presses his pink nose
to the door of his cage
and decides for the fifty six
millionth time
that he can't get
through it.

Our hamster's life:
there's not much
to it,
not much
to it.

It's about the most boring
life in the world,
if he only
knew it.
He sleeps and he drinks and he eats.
He eats and he drinks and he sleeps.

He slinks and he dreeps.
He eats.

This process
he repeats.

Our hamster's life:
there's not much
to it,
not much
to it.

You'd think it would drive him bonkers,
going round and round on his wheel.
It's certainly driving me bonkers,

watching him
do it.

But he may be thinking:
'That boy's life,
there's not much
to it,
not much
to it:

watching a hamster go round on a wheel.
It's driving me bonkers if he only knew it,

watching him
watching me
do it.'

Jeremy Mobster Lobster

In the black salt-sluices of the weed-choked rockpool
    With fish-eyes, garbage, vanishing fry
And rusting backbones in the squelchy tunnel
    That opens and closes like a murderous eye
    As the tide slurs in and the tide drawls out
    And the grinding shingle churns about,
            With his horrible claws
                For company
            Sits Jeremy Mobster Lobster,
            The meanest fish in the sea.

        The meanest fish,
        The uncleanest fish,
        The obscenest fish in the sea.

Watch out, shrimp! Better say your prayers!
Down in the rockpool
Jeremy's God.
Better have a little bit of
Dead fish ready
For that big mean old
Arth-ro-pod!

Pay up, crayfish! Pay up, crab!
Shell out for Jeremy's
Protection racket.
It'll cost you a packet
But don't complain

Or you might not grow
That shell again . . .

His wavering, wobbly, flickering eye-stalks
    Scrape round the walls of his bony cave
And you'll find no cover in the wallowing darkness,
    You won't be hidden by the blackest wave
    For there with the barnacles studding his back
    And you in mind as his next big snack,
        With his horrible claws
            For company
        Sits Jeremy Mobster Lobster,
        The meanest fish in the sea.

*   The meanest fish,*
*   The uncleanest fish,*
*   The obscenest fish in the sea.*

The Thumb Bird*

The storm beats down
    And the thumb bird flies
High above the ocean
    Where the great whales go:

Tiniest of little ones
    That wing the skies,
Love light your journey
    When the wild winds blow . . .

And the thumb bird flies . . .
    And the thumb bird flies
        Far across the sea . . .

All among the pine trees
    She will make her nest
From moss and feathers
    In a cobweb sewn,

Till with her tiny ones
   She is blessed:
Love light their journey
   When they fly alone . . .

And the thumb bird flies . . .
   And the thumb bird flies
     Far across the sea . . .

Snuggled in the feathers
   On the woodcock's back.
Taking a ride
   On her way across the deep:

Though thunder roll
   And lightning crack,
Love light your journey
   Till you safely sleep . . .

And the thumb bird's flown . . .
   And the thumb bird's flown
     Far across the sea.

* A name for the goldcrest, Britain's smallest bird

Of Me and You and All of Us

Nothing Else

There's nothing I can't see
From here.

There's nothing I can't be
From here.

Because my eyes
Are open wide
To let the big
World come inside,

I think I can see me
From here.

Me

My Mum is on a diet,
My Dad is on the booze,
My Gran's out playing Bingo
And she was born to lose.

My brother's stripped his motorbike
Although it's bound to rain.
My sister's playing Elton John
Over and over again.

What a dim old family!
What a dreary lot!
Sometimes I think that I'm the only
Superstar they've got.

How I See It

Some say the world's
A hopeless case:
A speck of dust
In all that space.
It's certainly
A scruffy place.
Just one hope
For the human race
That I can see:
Me. I'm
ACE!

Not Known at This Address

I decided to ask my friends to write,
If ever they would, instead of just
Talk talk talk,

To:

THE DEPARTMENT OF HUMAN GENIUS,
CENTRE OF WORLD EXCELLENCE,
73 MILL WALK.

And one of them
Actually did. My mum
Had carefully placed the envelope
On the windowsill.
She said:

'That seems to be for you.
I think it's a bill.'

Mirror Poem

If I look within the mirror,
Deep inside its frozen tears,
Shall I see the man I'll marry
Standing at my shoulder,
    Leaning down the years?

Shall I smile upon the mirror,
Shall my love look, smiling, back?
Midnight on Midsummer's eve:
What becomes of marriage
    If the glass should crack?

I Don't Like You

If I were the Prime Minister of Britain
And you were a snail,
I'd be most careful walking round my garden
Not to disturb your trail.

If I were a snail and you were the Prime Minister,
It wouldn't be like that.
You'd tramp around in your expensive boots
And squash me flat.

I Like You

When you're unkind
You don't mean to be.
And when you're kind
You couldn't care less
Whether or not
You're seen to be.

What I like about you
Is how you know what's cooking
In somebody else's mind.
You do the best you can
And you just don't care
Who's looking.

All of Us

All of us are afraid
More often than we tell.

There are times we cling like mussels to the sea-wall,
And pray that the pounding waves
Won't smash our shell.

Times we hear nothing but the sound
Of our loneliness, like a cracked bell
From fields far away where the trees are in icy shade.

O many a time in the night-time and in the day,
More often than we say,
We are afraid.

If people say they are never frightened,
I don't believe them.
If people say they are frightened,
I want to retrieve them

From that dark shivering haunt
Where they don't want to be,
Nor I.

Let's make of ourselves, therefore, an enormous sky
Over whatever
We most hold dear.

And we'll comfort each other,
Comfort each other's
Fear.

January Birth
(for Caroline Maclean)

Brightest splinter, scarlet berry,
  On the shivered world you lay,
Sliver from the tree of winter
  When the hawthorn held no may,
When the city plane was childless
  And the dark was in the day.

From her labour then your mother
  Freely wept to see you wake,
Take this crying star for neighbour:
  Wept with joy for your fierce sake,
Heart of light in snowing darkness,
  Storm of love and glistening flake.

O tender head, bare tree that branches
  Veins in perilous array,
May the violent day defend you.
  Want for nothing, little clay.
O cup of air, O moth-light wingbeat,
  Darling, bear the world away.

Trade Secrets

In Memory of a Beautiful Jeweller

Within the crescent of your jeweller's bench,
Nothing of all the intricate things you made
More beautiful than the shining
Necklace of your laughter,

Linking the days. Within the days,

Nothing of any rarer,
More precious metal than were you,
Loving and strong and brave
And capable and true.

The Woodman's Axe

The old woodman had only one axe,
a true axe and a keen one.
He swung it in the oakwood
all day long.

When the handle split he fitted another.
When the blade cracked he fitted another.
He passed it on to his son,
who swung it in the oakwood
all day long.

Blade and handle, handle and blade,
he fitted as he needed.

A man said, 'What is left of the axe
whose parts have changed so many times?'

But the son said, 'I have only one axe
passed on to me by my father:
a true axe and a keen one.'

And he passed it on to his son.

Say 'Aagh!'

No fun being the dentist.
  Not much fun as a job:
Spending all of your days in gazing
  Right into everyone's gob.

No fun *seeing* the dentist.
  Not much fun at all:
Staring straight up his hairy nostrils –
  Drives you up the wall!

Watch Out, Walter Wall!

The king of carpet salesmen
   Is a man called Walter Wall.
He's got a shop next door to us
   He used to think too small.
And so he asked permission, please,
   To *alter* WALTER WALL.

'What? Alter WALTER WALL?' the Council
   Cried. 'Why? What's the call?'
'My rugs are filling up with bugs
   From standing in the hall.
My place has got no stacking-space –
   No space,' said Walt, 'at all!'

The Council said, 'Go right ahead.
   Don't falter, Walter Wall!
It's alteration stations, Walter.
   Sideways, build a tall
Extension, that will form an extra
   Wall to WALTER WALL!'

And so across the taller wall
   I call to Walter Wall
And over it I often boot
   A ball to Walter Wall.
Likewise the cat can crawl the wall
   And *fall* to Walter Wall!

So everything has worked out well:
  More space for Walter Wall.
The cat and I have got a place
  To crawl, fall, boot a ball:

And often, I am proud to say,
  The cat and ball, instead
Of landing on the carpets, clout
  Old Walt *hard* on the head!

Sid the Rat

Sid was a rat
Who kept a hat shop,
Ordinary sort of stuff:

Pork pies,
Panamas,
Old flat caps,
Bowlers,
Boaters
For old fat chaps,
Deerstalkers,
Stetsons . . .
And that was *enough*
For *that* shop!

Yes, Sid was a rat
Who kept a hat shop,
Ordinary sort of trade:

Eels,
Elks,
Dirty old foxes,
Skinny
Kittens
In travelling boxes,
Elephants,
Owls . . .
And business *paid*
In *that* shop!

One day the Mayor knocked on the door,
Said, 'Sid, you can't stay here no more!
We're going to knock your hat shop down
To build a new road through the town!'

'Is that a fact?'
Said Sid the Rat,
'Is that a fact?'
Said he.
'We'll see!

You build your road and I'll get my hats,
And I'll stack them up like a block of flats

Right in the middle
And, hey-diddle-diddle,
The cars won't know
Which way to go!
And I'll get the elk,
And the dirty old fox,
And the kitten
Out of her travelling box,
And the slithering eel,
And the wise owl too,
And the elephant
On his way to the zoo,
And I'll tell you what they'll do!

They'll pull those drivers out,
Willy-nilly,
And they'll tickle those drivers
And tickle them silly!
There'll be *huge* traffic jams
But they won't care!
So how do you like *that*,
Mr Mayor?'

'Oh,' said the Mayor.
'Oh dear,' said the Mayor.
'Hum,' said the Mayor.
'I fear,' said the Mayor,
'You'd better keep your hat shop, Sid,
And carry on the way you did!'

Sid

Did!

The Fate of the Supermarket Manager

There once was a Supermarket manager
And a very happy manager was he.

He *reduced the prices*
Of the lollies and the ices!
He made *huge cuts*
On the fruit and nuts!
Corn-flakes, steaks
And home-bake cakes,
Dog-food, detergent,
Devil-fish, dates,
He sold at *half*
The market rates!
And (so my sister
Said to me)
He put stickers
On the knickers
In the Lingerie
Saying:
Prices down
By 15p!
And he wrote, as a treat,
By the luncheon meat:
YOU'D HAVE TO BE BARMY
TO BUY THIS SALAMI
So he gave it away
For free!

Yes, there once was a Supermarket manager
And a very happy manager was he.

What a bloke!

He was much admired.

The shop went broke.

He was fired.

Song Sung by a Man on a Barge to Another Man on a Different Barge in Order to Drive Him Mad

Oh,

I am the best bargee bar none,
You are the best bargee bar one!
You are the second-best bargee,
You are the best bargee bar me!

Oh,

I am the best . . .

(and so on, until he is
hurled into the canal)

Family Failings

Hugger Mugger

I'd sooner be
Jumped and thumped and dumped,

I'd sooner be
Slugged and mugged . . . than *hugged* . . .

And clobbered with a slobbering
Kiss by my Auntie Jean:

You know what I mean:

Whenever she comes to stay,
You know you're bound

To get one.
A quick
   short
   peck
   would
   be
   OK
But this is a
Whacking great
Smacking great
Wet one!

All whoosh and spit
And crunch and squeeze
And '*Dear* little boy!'

And 'Auntie's missed you!'
And 'Come to Auntie, she
Hasn't *kissed* you!'
Please don't do it, Auntie,
PLEASE!

Or if you've absolutely
Got to,

And nothing on *earth* can persuade you
Not to,

The trick
Is to make it
Quick,

You know what I mean?

For as things are,
I really would far,

Far sooner be
Jumped and thumped and dumped,

I'd sooner be
Slugged and mugged . . . than *hugged* . . .

And clobbered with a slobbering
Kiss by my Auntie

Jean!

Uncle Know-all

He knows what's what,
He knows what's not,
He knows that never
The twain shall meet.
He knows his onions,
He knows his bunions,
He knows his nose
And he knows his feet.

He knows his mind,
He knows his value,
Knows what happens,
Knows how it goes.
He knows the lot
And doesn't he love it,
I wish he'd shove it
Up his nose!

Dad's Beard

Last year my Dad grew a great big thick red beard:
Mum made him.
Can't think how in the world she managed
To persuade him.

   Nothing but hair
   Everywhere:
      Can't say I liked it at all.

But now he's shaved it,
I wonder:
Should he have saved it?

It's odd. Did Dad look better with his beard?
I doubt it.
But he certainly looks pretty weird
Without it.

   Nothing but face
   All over the place:
      Can't say I like it at all.

Where the Flowers Went

Where have all the flowers gone,
The flowers that were standing on
The grave beside the churchyard wall?
    My little brother grabbed them

And stuffed them in an old tin can
And took them home to give my Gran,
Who wasn't very pleased at all –
    'Tell me where you nabbed them!'

    Then out they crept
    As quiet as mice

    To put them back
    Without being caught:

    'It's *wrong*,' said Gran,
    'But still the thought

Was

Nice!'

Moodswings and Mindbends

The Sea in the Trees

When the warm wind was flowing
In the leaves of the tall ash tree,
The old man fell asleep in the park
And he dreamed the sound of the sea.

The branches filled and billowed,
The high mainmast swayed,
As long sea-miles of the afternoon
His green galleon made . . .

In the harbour of the shade.

Some Days

I didn't find it interesting,
Listening,
I didn't find it interesting,
Talking,
So I left the house – I went miles and miles –
And I didn't find it interesting,
Walking.

I didn't find it interesting,
Reading,
I didn't find it interesting,
Writing,
So I left the house – I went miles and miles –
And that wasn't terribly
Exciting.

I watched my sister playing
Patience,
But I didn't find it interesting,
Scoring,
So I left the house – I went miles and miles –
And that was *extremely*
Boring.

I didn't find it interesting,
Telly,
There wasn't much on
That night,
So I sat in a chair and I went to sleep . . .
A dull old day
All right.

All of the Morning

I've been staring
  all of the morning
    out at the endlessly
     falling rain

that drowns the garden
  in tank after tank full
    of see-through tears without
     anger or pain,

joy or sorrow,
  shock or laughter,
    only the helplessly
     falling rain

that springs pink worms
  from their tight dark prison
    and sticks the snails
      to the bumpy wall

with what appear to be
  squiggles of stretched, spat,
    chewed-up chewing-gum.
      Let it fall,

flooding the cones
  of lilac, laburnum's
    yellow bells
      that ring their small

tune of the sun
  in the soaked grey morning,
    let it fall.
      If I weren't me,

the helpless rain
  that falls forever
    I could be,
      quite easily.

Bluebells and Penguins

The day we found the lady
Crying in the wood
We tried to comfort her
As best we could
But just what she was crying for
We never understood:

Weeping among the beechleaves and the bluebells.

The day we saw the old man
Cackling at the zoo
We had a laugh along with him
The way you do
But just what he was laughing at
We never had a clue:

Chuckling among the pythons and the penguins!

Now penguins aren't that funny
And bluebells aren't that sad
But sometimes you feel really good
And sometimes you feel bad.
Sometimes you feel sky-high happy,
Sometimes lost and low,
And why on earth you feel like that
Sometimes
    you
       don't
          know!

Did You Ever!

Did you ever
Meet an old man in a sky-blue overcoat?
Yes? Well, so did I.

    Hat on his head,
    Hands on his knees,
    Beard on his face,
    Pipe in his mouth
    And a look in his eye
    That said:
    'I may not be too clever, folks,
    But goodness knows, I try!'

You met him and so did I.

Did you ever
Meet an old woman in a sharkskin waistcoat?
Yes? Well, so did I.

    Cap on her head,
    Freckles on her knees,
    Grin on her face,
    Twig in her mouth
    And a look in her eye
    That said:
    'I'm feeling frisky as a two-week kitten,
    Somebody tell me why!'

You met her and so did I.

Did you ever
Meet an old dog in velvet trousers?
Never? Neither did I.

It's Spring, It's Spring

It's spring, it's spring –

when everyone sits round a roaring fire
telling ghost stories!

It's spring, it's spring –

when everyone sneaks into everyone else's yard
and bashes up their snowman!

It's spring, it's spring –

when the last dead leaves fall from the trees
and Granny falls off your toboggan!

It's spring, it's spring –

when you'd give your right arm
for a steaming hot bowl of soup!

It's spring, it's spring –

when you'd give your right leg
not to be made to wash up after Christmas dinner!

It's spring, it's spring –

isn't it?

It's Winter, It's Winter

It's winter, it's winter, it's wonderful winter,
When everyone lounges around in the sun!

It's winter, it's winter, it's wonderful winter,
When everyone's brown like a steak overdone!

It's winter, it's winter, it's wonderful winter,
It's swimming and surfing and hunting for
   conkers!

It's winter, it's winter, it's wonderful winter,
And I am completely and utterly bonkers!

March Dusk

About the hour light wobbles
Between the day and night,

On paving-stones and cobbles
Rain hisses with weak spite

And plane trees, dangling bobbles,
Drip leafless from numb height

Where wounded springtime hobbles
That soon will leap with light.

Acorn Haiku

Just a green olive
In its own little egg-cup:
It can feed the sky.

Dream On

Hundreds and Thousands

Under the hair-drier,
Under the hair,

The head of my sister
Is dreaming of where

She sits by the sea-shore
On somebody's yacht,

Drinking and thinking
And dreaming of what

She'll buy with her hundreds
And thousands of dollars,

Like ten silver tom-cats
With golden flea-collars

To yawn round the lawn
Of her garden in France

Where she lies by the pool
As the blue ripples dance,

And millions of brilliant
People dive in,

All loaded with money
And honey and gin,

All wonderfully funny
With witty remarks

As the sun in the water
Makes shivering sparks

And there by the pool
She lies browning and basking as

All of the people cry,
'Thank you for asking us!'

That's what I read
In her dopey sea-stare

Under the hair-drier,
Under the hair.

She wakes from her dreaming
Of making a mint

And – *would you believe it?* –
She's UTTERLY SKINT!

She's stealing all *my*
Pocket money from *me*!

'I'm off to the Disco –
Need 20 more p!'

Dreadful Dream

I'm glad to say
I've never met
A cannibal
And yet

In this dream
I had last night
I almost took
A bite

Of somebody
Or other who
Was standing in
A stew-

Pot full of water
On a batch
Of firewood. Just
One match

Would do to start
It off. Whereat
I hollered, 'Just
Stop that!'

But cannibals
Began to shout:
'You've got to try
Him out!'

'Who? Me?' 'That's right.'
'I'd rather not,'
I said. They yelled,
'You've *got*

To have a taste!
Don't *want* to?' 'Not,'
I answered them,
'A lot,

Since, now you put
Me on the spot,
He wouldn't taste
So hot.'

At this the chap
Who'd soon be stewed
Remarked, 'I call
That *rude*!

Most ungrateful!
Here I am –
About to be
A ham –

Just to *please* you!
"WHAT A TREAT",
Not "HE'S UNFIT
TO EAT",

Is what I'd hoped
To hear. Well, stuff

It then, I've had
Enough.'

And out he stepped
As bold as day,
Shook-dried and stalked
Away.

The cannibals got
Quite excited:
'Last time *you're*
Invited!

Could have had him
On a bun:
Now look what
You've done!

Hurt his feelings,
BUNGLEHEAD!
We'll eat *you*
Instead.'

Things had got
Beyond a joke.
Thank goodness I
Awoke.

Dreadful dream!
Next time I sleep,
I plan to do
It deep.

Blue Wish

When the gas-fire glows
　It tingles with a
　　　Low
　　Blue light.
　　　It
Dances with a slow
　Flicker of wishing:
Wish I may,
　Wish I might

Have a blue wish
　Always burning,
Noon,
　Burning,
　　　Night.

Dragonella . . .

Ella was feeling poorly.
Ella stayed home in bed.
She couldn't go out
And she couldn't play,
She couldn't have fun
With her friends that day,
So Ella's mother
Read a story
Just for her,
Instead.

But the story was rather *boring* . . .
      The story wasn't much good.
So Ella stared through the window
      At the garden beside the wood . . .

And there was a bonfire burning
      With little tongues of flame
Flickering underneath it,
      And Ella dreamed she became . . .

Something very strange indeed:
A creature of *quite* a different breed!

She felt her shoulders were suddenly sprouting wings,
And her feet turned into claws,
And a battering tail went clattering out behind her . . .
While her breathing came in fiery snorts and roars . . .

DRAGONELLA she was!
Beating her strange new wings!
Breathing fire in the winter sky,
High above
   All living things . . .

Then Dragonella went flying over a forest.
She saw in a clearing between the trees
A very old couple who looked so sad
That she dropped down beside them
Upon her knees.

'We're very, *very cold*,' the old folks said,
'Our fire's gone out and it just won't light.'
'Leave it to me!' said Dragonella.
She blew . . . and she blew . . .
With all her might . . .

And the fire flamed up
   In a golden storm . . .
Those very old folks
   Felt nice and warm!

Then Dragonella went running on through the wood,
And the wood grew darker,
The wood grew dimmer . . .
But there was *just*
Enough of a glimmer . . .

For her to see a wizard crawling
Among the leaves, and she heard him calling,
'Where, oh where is my wonderful wand?
It's a wand of which
I was very, very fond,
But I've put it down and I can't think where . . .
And it's much too *dark* to find it here!'

Then Dragonella blew out a stream of flame
    And the wizard cried, 'I can see it now!
Oh thank you! I just can't *tell* you how
    Glad I am you came!'

And then she took to the air again on her wings,

And soon she was flying
High over the sea . . .
When . . . goodness me,
Beneath her was one of the most amazing things!

    A lady was chained
    To the rocks below,
    And the sea was rising:
    'Oh no, no, no!'
    Cried Dragonella,
    And down she flew
    To see what she
    Could do . . .

And there stood a nasty old giant who'd chained up the
    lady,
Looking as mean as mean could be.
So Dragonella gave him a whack
With her battering tail. 'Now, don't come back!'
She yelled as he fell down into the swirling sea . . .

Then she breathed out a wonderful crimson wave of fire

That melted the chains, so the lady was free
To jump on Dragonella's back,
And they both went flying above the foam . . .
And when they were over the forest again,
The lady cried, 'That's my home!'

For the very old folks were her father and mother . . .
And the wizard, her rather peculiar brother!
So when those two dropped down from the sky,
Everyone hugged and hugged each other,

Until
    It was time
To say
    Goodbye . . .

As Dragonella went flying back over the sea,
A very different thing she began to be . . .

And Ella woke
    In her nice warm bed.
'Did you like that story?'
    Her mother said.

'You look much better!
And where did you find
That beautiful golden
Bracelet chain?
It feels so *warm*!'
'Well . . .
Never you mind . . .'

Said Ella!

The Magic Box

I will put in my box

the swish of a silk sari on a summer night,
fire from the nostrils of a Chinese dragon,
the hidden pass that steals through the mountains.

I will put in the box

a snowman with a rumbling belly,
a sip of the bluest water from Lake Lucerne,
a leaping spark from an electric fish.

I will put in the box

three violet wishes spoken in Gujarati,
the last joke of an ancient uncle
and the first smile of a baby.

I will put in the box

a fifth season and a black sun,
a cowboy on a broomstick
and a witch on a white horse.

My box is fashioned from ice and gold and steel,
with stars on the lid and secrets in the corners.
Its hinges are the toe joints
of dinosaurs.

I shall surf on my box on the great
high-rolling breakers of the wild Atlantic,
then wash ashore on a yellow beach
the colour of the sun.

Tigerella

Ella was nice at the barbecue party,
Everything Ella did
Was right.

She handed round the sausages
And *didn't* give
The dog a fright.

She didn't tease the old tom cat
Or stamp on old Mr Rathbone's hat,
She never, ever did things like that

As *some*
Would have thought
She might.

No,

Ella was *fine* at the barbecue party,
Ella was
Quite all right!

Good as gold and nice as pie,
She sweetly kissed each guest goodbye
And they all said, 'Ella, it's been a pleasure!
Ella, *aren't* you a little treasure!
We're just so sorry we have to go!'

But
      Little
            Did
                  They
                        Know . . .

They didn't know at all
That at the midnight stroke
Ella stirred in her bed
And a changed Ella woke

With a furry kind of growl
And hide of yellow and black
And whiskers and golden eyes
And a TAIL at the end of her back!

Softly she loped down the midnight stairs,
In the breathing dark her eyes shone bright,
And she poured herself from the open window
Onto the lawn in the mad moonlight.

TIGERELLA she was!
TIGERELLA her name!
A giant cat of the jungle
By moonlight she became!

Rippling over the silver grass
(She left no mark, she made no sound),
On she moved with flowing shoulders,
Wild One on the midnight ground.

Easily as her shadow
She glided over the wall.
She raised her head in the cornfield,
Seeing, scenting all . . .

And then she was gathering pace through the whispering
        barley,
Running, racing, the beat of her heart in tune
With the earth and the night and the creatures until she
        coiled
And LEAPT and bit a piece from the rolling moon!

She cuffed the stars about!
Tigerella at play!

How she biffed them,
How she battered them,

How she skittered them,
How she scattered them

Up and down
The Milky Way!

And soon through the bright star-clusters
She was travelling on;
By glittering constellations,
She sailed
              At the side
                    Of the Swan . . .

Over the great calm lake of space . . .

Until she soared and, face to face
And paw to paw, she found the Bear
And they jumbled and tumbled everywhere,
They tussled and hustled, wrestled and nestled,
Two beasts playing together there!

But Mighty Orion the Hunter
Gazed at the stars below.

Mighty Orion the Hunter
Raised his shimmering bow.

He sent an arrow whizzing
Down like a silver streak

Through the billion bits of the heavens
And grazed Tigerella's cheek!

So Tigerella turned
And raced it in its track.

She caught it and she wheeled
And hurled that arrow back!

And then they were diving down through the huge
    unknown.
Wild star-cities they touched and they tumbled beyond,
As they fell through the brain of the night until they
    landed
On tingling paws

By Ella's
Garden
Pond!

They lapped the water. They licked each other's face.
'See you again,' they said. 'So long. Take care.'

Then Tigerella poured herself in through the window,
And up to his home in the heavens soared the Bear . . .

Ella was nice and polite at breakfast,
Ella sat primly
At her place.

Her mother said, 'Ella,
Did you sleep all right, dear?
What's that scratch there
On your face?'

Ella said, 'Naughty old Tom-cat did it!'
'Did he? The wicked old
So-and-so!'

'Yes,' said Ella, 'Yes, he did!'
And
    Little
        Did
            They
                Know!

Talkative Types

Rabbiting On

Where did you go?
Oh . . . nowhere much.

What did you see?
Oh . . . rabbits and such.

Rabbits? What else?
Oh . . . a rabbit hutch.

What sort of rabbits?
What sort? Oh . . . small.

What sort of hutch?
Just a hutch, that's all.

But what did it look like?
Like a rabbit hutch.

Well, what was in it?
Small rabbits and such.

I worried about you
While you were gone.

*Why don't you stop
Rabbiting on?*

Rabbiting Off

Now you see me,
Now you don't,
First you'll miss me,
Then you won't.

Spoken my story,
Sung my song.
I've been round here
All day long

For a yell and a whisper,
Shout and a cough,
Rabbiting on
And sounding off.

Sounding off
And rabbiting on:
I was here
And now I'm . . .

Babbling and Gabbling

My Granny's an absolute corker,
My Granny's an absolute cracker,
But she's Britain's speediest talker
And champion yackety-yacker!

Everyone's fond of my Granny,
Everyone thinks she's nice,
But before you can say Jack Robinson,
My Granny's said it twice!

Gobbling and Squabbling

In a very old house
On a street full of cobbles,
Two very old ladies
Have got colly-wobbles,

And out on the pavement
The neighbours are grumbling,
And sighing, 'Oh *when* will
Their stomachs stop rumbling?'

Laurie and Dorrie

The first thing that you'll notice if
    You meet my Uncle Laurie
Is how, whatever else he does,
    He can't stop saying sorry.

He springs from bed at 5 a.m.
    As birds begin to waken,
Cries, 'No offence intended, lads –
    Likewise, I hope, none taken!'

This drives his wife, my Auntie Dorrie,
    Mad. It's not surprising
She grabs him by the throat and screeches,
    'Stop apologizing!'

My Uncle, who's a little deaf,
    Says, 'Sorry? Sorry, Dorrie?'
'For goodness' sake,' Aunt Dorrie screams,
    'Stop saying sorry, Laurie!'

'Sorry, dear? Stop saying what?'
    'SORRY!' Laurie's shaken.
'No need to be, my dear,' he says,
    'For *no offence is taken.*

Likewise I'm sure that there was none
    Intended on your part.'
'Dear Lord,' Aunt Dorrie breathes, 'what can
    I do, where do I start?'

Then, 'Oh, I *see*,' says Uncle L.,
   'You mean "stop saying sorry"!
I'm sorry to have caused offence –
   Oops! Er . . . *sorry*, Dorrie!'

The Song of the Whale

Heaving mountain in the sea,
Whale, I heard you
Grieving.

Great whale, crying for your life,
Crying for your kind, I knew
How we would use
Your dying:

Lipstick for our painted faces,
Polish for our shoes.

Tumbling mountain in the sea,
Whale, I heard you
Calling.

Bird-high notes, keening, soaring:
At their edge a tiny drum
Like a heartbeat.

We would make you
Dumb.

In the forest of the sea,
Whale, I heard you
Singing,

Singing to your kind.
We'll never let you be.
Instead of life we choose

Lipstick for our painted faces,
Polish for our shoes.

Whisper Whisper

whisper whisper
whisper whisper
goes my sister
down the phone

whisper whisper
go the beech leaves
breathing in the
wind alone

whisper whisper
whisper whisper
slips the river
on the stone

whisper whisper
go my parents
when they whisper
on their own

I don't mind the
whisper whisper
whisper whisper
it's a tune

sometimes though
I wish the whisper
whisperings would
shut up soon

Waiting for the Tone

My sister is my surest friend
And yet, GREAT SNAKES! she seems to spend
Her *life* upon the telephone
Talking to her boyfriend, Tone,
Although – a sad and sorry joke –
She doesn't seem to like the bloke.

> *'Don't take that tone with me, Tone,*
> *Don't take that tone with me,*
> *Or else I'll put down the phone, Tone,*
> *And alone, Tone, you will be.*

> *'Don't call me just to moan, Tone,*
> *Can't stand your whingeing on.*
> *Next time you ring for a groan, Tone,*
> *You'll find that I have gone.'*

And she can keep this up for hours:
Her taste for Tone's moans never sours.
So when I think that he might call
I silently steal down the hall
And give the phone a hateful look . . .
Then take the blighter off the hook.

Watch Your French

When my mum tipped a panful of red-hot fat
Over her foot, she did quite a little chat,
And I won't tell you what she said
But it wasn't:
'Fancy that!
I must try in future to be far more careful
With this red-hot scalding fat!'

When my dad fell over and landed – splat! –
With a trayful of drinks (he'd tripped over the cat)
I won't tell you what he said
But it wasn't:
'Fancy that!
I must try in future to be far more careful
To step *round* our splendid cat!'

When Uncle Joe brought me a cowboy hat
Back from the States, the dog stomped it flat,
And I won't tell you what I said
But Mum and Dad yelled:
'STOP THAT!
Where did you learn that appalling language?
Come on. Where?'

'I've no idea,' I said,
'No idea.'

My Dad, Your Dad

My dad's fatter than your dad,
Yes, my dad's fatter than yours:
If he eats any more he won't fit in the house,
He'll have to live out of doors.

Yes, but my dad's balder than your dad,
My dad's balder, OK,
He's only got two hairs left on his head
And both are turning grey.

Ah, but my dad's thicker than your dad,
My dad's thicker, all right.
He has to look at his watch to see
If it's noon or the middle of the night.

Yes, but my dad's more boring than your dad.
If he ever starts counting sheep
When he can't get to sleep at night, he finds
It's the sheep that go to sleep.

But my dad doesn't mind your dad.
Mine quite likes yours too.
I suppose they don't always think much of US!
That's true, I suppose, that's true.

Lies

When we are bored
My friend and I
Tell
Lies.

It's a competition: the prize
Is won by the one
Whose lies
Are the bigger size.

We really do:
That's true.
But there isn't a prize:
That's lies.

How to Treat the House-plants

All she ever thinks about are house-plants.
She talks to them and tends them every day.
And she says, 'Don't hurt their feelings. Give them
Love. In all your dealings with them,
Treat them in a tender, *human* way.'

'Certainly, my dear,' he says. 'OK.
Human, eh?'

But the house-plants do not seem to want to play.

They are stooping, they are drooping,
They are kneeling in their clay:
They are flaking, they are moulting,
Turning yellow, turning grey,
And they look . . . well, quite revolting
As they sigh, and fade away.

So after she has left the house he gets them
And he sets them in a line against the wall,
And I cannot say he cossets them or pets them –
No, he doesn't sympathize with them at all.
Is he tender? Is he human? Not a bit.
No, to each of them in turn he says: 'You *twit*!

   You're a
      Rotten little skiver,
      Cost a fiver,
      Earn your keep!

You're a
>Dirty little drop-out!
>You're a cop-out!
>You're a creep!

You're a
>Mangy little whinger!
>You're a cringer!
>Son, it's true –

>I have justbin
>To the dustbin
>Where there's *better men than you*!

>Get that stem back!

>Pull your weight!

>Stick your leaves out!

>STAND UP STRAIGHT!'

And, strange to say, the plants co-operate.
So when she comes back home and finds them glowing,
Green and healthy, every one a king,
She says, 'It's *tenderness* that gets them growing!
How strange, the change a little love can bring!'

'Oh yes,' he says. 'Not half. Right. Love's the thing.'

The Orbison Consolations

Only the lonely
Know the way you feel tonight?
Surely the poorly
Have *some* insight?
Oddly, the godly
Also might,
And slowly the lowly
Will learn to read you right.

Simply the pimply
Have some idea.
Quaintly the saintly
Have got quite near.
Quickly the sickly
Empathize
And prob'ly the knobbly
Look deep into your eyes.

Rumly, the comely
Will understand.
Shortly the portly
Will take your hand.
Early the surly
Dispraised and panned,
But lately the stately
Have joined your saraband.

Only the lonely
Know the way you feel tonight?
Singly the tingly
Conceive your plight,
But *doubly* the bubbly
Fly your kite . . .

And lastly the ghastly
Know the way you feel tonight.

News from the Pews
and Other Views

The Wicked Singers

And have you been out carol singing,
Collecting for the Old Folk's Dinner?

Oh yes indeed, oh yes indeed.

And did you sing all the Christmas numbers,
Every one a winner?

Oh yes indeed, oh yes indeed.

Good King Wenceslas, and Hark
The Herald Angels Sing?

Oh yes indeed, oh yes indeed.

And did you sing them loud and clear
And make the night sky ring?

Oh yes indeed, oh yes indeed.

And did you count up all the money?
Was it quite a lot?

Oh yes indeed, oh yes indeed.

And did you give it all to the Vicar,
Everything you'd got?

Certainly not, certainly not.

Fair Warning of a Goddess

She can change her shape
To a snake or a sparrow,
With a silver arrow
Shoot down the moon:
She can tickle the sun
Awake at night-time,
Tip over darkness
Into noon.

She'll come yesterday,
She was here tomorrow,
She can bend and borrow
Whale words from the sea:
With one big toe
She can stop a river
Dead, then hang it
Up on a tree.

She can spin the world
On a single finger
And make life linger
Or let it go:
She can char the sky
With a wedding torch
Or from one dead branch
Make a forest grow:

If you should meet her
In TAMILNADU,
Don't say I didn't ever
Tell you so . . .

When the Pope Takes a Shower

Should the Pope
grope
for the soap,
and the soap
slip off the slope,
would the Pope
feel a dope,
would hope
be beyond his scope,
would the Pope
mope?

Nope.
The Pope
could cope.

Zoob

I
am
ZOOB.

You can't fit me
in a triangle, a circle
or a cube.

I'm the empty seat beside you
on the 31 bus
or the Tube.

If you think you can describe me,
let me tell you that
you're making a
BOOB.

I can see round corners,
I can look in your eyes.
You can't see me,
but I'm wondrous wise.

I'm ZOOB.

That's whoob.

I'm what the wind means
when it moans,
'Zoob . . . Zoob.'

I'm what the sky says
when it groans,
'Zoob . . . Zoob.'

I'm as near as you are,
I'm as far as the sun,
I'm everything
And I am one:

I'm youb . . .

Zoob . . .

ZOOB . . .

ZOOB . . .

What Went Wrong at My Sister's Wedding

The bridegroom was supposed
To kiss the bride,
Not kick 'er

And

He shouldn't have kissed
The Vicar

And

They should have thrown
Confetti,
Not

Spaghetti.

A Boy Called
Dave Dirt

My Party

My parents said I could have a party
And that's just what I did.

Dad said, 'Who had you thought of inviting?'
I told him. He said, 'Well, you'd better start writing,'
And that's just what I did

To:
Phyllis Willis, Horace Morris,
Nancy, Clancy, Bert and Gert Sturt,
Dick and Mick and Nick Crick,
Ron, Don, John,
Dolly, Molly, Polly –
Neil Peel –
And my dear old friend, Dave Dirt.

I wrote, 'Come along, I'm having a party,'
And that's just what they did.

They all arrived with huge appetites
As Dad and I were fixing the lights.
I said, 'Help yourself to the drinks and bites!'
And that's just what they did,
All of them:

Phyllis Willis, Horace Morris,
Nancy, Clancy, Bert and Gert Sturt,
Dick and Mick and Nick Crick,
Ron, Don, John,
Dolly, Molly, Polly –
Neil Peel –
And my dear old friend, Dave Dirt.

Now, I had a good time and as far as I could tell,
The party seemed to go pretty well –
Yes, that's just what it did.

Then Dad said, 'Come on, just for fun,
Let's have a *turn* from everyone!'
And a turn's just what they did,

All of them:

Phyllis Willis, Horace Morris,
Nancy, Clancy, Bert and Gert Sturt,
Dick and Mick and Nick Crick,
Ron, Don, John,
Dolly, Molly, Polly –
Neil Peel –
And my dear old friend, Dave Dirt.

AND THIS IS WHAT THEY DID:

Phyllis and Clancy
And Horace and Nancy
Did a song and dance number
That was really fancy –

Dolly, Molly, Polly,
Ron, Don and John
Performed a play
That went on and on and on –

Gert and Bert Sturt,
Sister and brother,
Did an imitation of
Each other.

(Gert Sturt put on Bert Sturt's shirt
And Bert Sturt put on Gert Sturt's skirt.)

Neil Peel
All on his own
Danced an eightsome reel.

Dick and Mick
And Nicholas Crick
Did a most *ingenious*
Conjuring trick

And my dear old friend, Dave Dirt,
Was terribly sick
All over the flowers.
We cleaned it up.
It took *hours*.

But as Dad said, giving a party's not easy.
You really
Have to
Stick at it.
I agree. And if Dave gives a party
I'm certainly
Going to be
Sick at it.

Dave Dirt Came to Dinner

Dave Dirt came to dinner
   And he stuck his chewing gum
Underneath the table
   And it didn't please my Mum

And it didn't please my Granny
   Who was quite a sight to see
When she got up from the table
   With the gum stuck to her knee

Where she put her cup and saucer
   When she sat and drank her tea
And the saucer and the chewing gum
   Got stuck as stuck can be

And she staggered round the kitchen
   With a saucer on her skirt –
No, it didn't please my Granny
   But it
      PLEASED
      DAVE
        DIRT

And the Dead
Are Walking

Ghosts

That's right. Sit down and talk to me.
What do you want to talk about?

Ghosts. You were saying that you believe in them.
Yes, they exist, without a doubt.

What, bony white nightmares that rattle and glow?
No, just spirits that come and go.

I've never heard such a load of rubbish.
Never mind, one day you'll know.

What makes you so sure?

I said:
What makes you so sure?

Hey,
Where did you go?

What Was It?

What was it
that could make
me wake
in the middle of the night
when the light
was a long way from coming
and the humming
of the fridge was the single
tingle
of sound
all round?

Why, when I crept downstairs and watched
green numbers sprinting on the kitchen clock,
was I afraid the empty rocking chair
might start to rock?

Why, when I stole back up and heard
the creak of each stair to my own
heart's quickening beats,

was I afraid that I should find
some other thing from the night outside
between my sheets?

Spooky Sentence

Outside was blind with mist till the grey turned darker
and swung its shadows from the beams

in the strange kitchen
where the old woman

sat with her head so low
between her pointy shoulders,

her chin was scooping for something I could not see
in the darkness lit by a tooth

and her grin
creaked . . .

In the Cathedral Gardens

In the Cathedral Gardens
Underneath the trees

In the chilly evening
The sun is on its knees,

Dying by the gravestones
While their shadows freeze

And the dead are walking
Underneath the trees.

I Heard Someone Crying

I heard someone crying
A long way off. I was going

Down Sampson Street. I was hoping
My sister would be staying.

She's living
A long way off from us, she's working

Somewhere else. That evening,
Coming

Home from school, I was turning
The key when I heard her laughing

And then she was kissing
My face and we were hugging

And tumbling. Who was crying
On Sampson Street?

Six White Skeletons

Deep deep down in the sea in the deep sea
    darkness
where the big fish
flicker and loom
and the weeds are alive
like hair

the hull of the wreck
grates in the sand:
in and out
of its ribs of steel –
only the long eel
moves there.

Down in the engine-room
six white skeletons:

only the long eel
moves there.

Mr Angelo

Mr Angelo's dead and gone,
And the worrying thought
Has entered my head:
How will the poor old man get on,
Him not speaking
A word of Dead?

Something He Left

An overcoat warming a clothes-hanger,
Alone in a cupboard after his body had gone
To be made into flame and memory,
Standing as still as he placed it,
Or very faintly trembling,
The night before the dawn he put death on.

Grandad

Grandad's dead
And I'm sorry about that.

He'd a huge black overcoat.
He felt proud in it.
You could have hidden
A football crowd in it.
Far too big –
It was a lousy fit
But Grandad didn't
Mind a bit.
He wore it all winter
With a squashed black hat.

Now he's dead
And I'm sorry about that.

He'd got twelve stories.
I'd heard every one of them
Hundreds of times
But that was the fun of them:
You knew what was coming
So you could join in.
He'd got big hands
And brown, grooved skin
And when he laughed
It knocked you flat.

Now he's dead
And I'm sorry about that.

Freeze

Pocked snow, cold-Christmas-pudding earth,
The tracery of winter trees,
The sky in danger with the dusk,
The mare's breath steaming in the freeze,

The sliding panes of river ice,
The olive water underneath,
The violet blade of last of light
That draws the darkness from its sheath.

Missing, 1944

My husband came stepping when I was a widow,
  My own one, my true love, all up to my door,
And he stood as a ghost in the freeze of the twilight,
  He stood in the body I'd never see more.

I knew he was gone and the Wellington bomber
  Came down in its fire to a grave in the sea,
My tears on his skin and the rock of his heartbeat,
  My dead love, my darling, is come home to me.

The Frozen Man

Out at the edge of town
where black trees

crack their fingers
in the icy wind

and hedges freeze
on their shadows

and the breath of cattle,
still as boulders,

hangs in rags
under the rolling moon,

a man is walking
alone:

on the coal-black road
his cold

feet
ring

and
ring.

Here in a snug house
at the heart of town

the fire is burning
red and yellow and gold:

you can hear the warmth
like a sleeping cat

breathe softly
in every room.

When the frozen man
comes to the door,

let him in,
let him in,
let him in.

Metal

A steelmill town, a ridge of pine,
  The taste of snow upon the tongue,
Meant all the world was black and white
  At Christmastime when he was young.

In softened angle, muted line,
  The harshnesses became oblique.
The keening lathes were pacified:
  All quiet on the frozen creek.

And it was Christmas when he died
  Far off, no place on earth to go,
But fresh as in his childhood came
  The scent of metal and of snow.

Mantles

White as the sacrament, in my grandmother's house the
    mantles
Were taught to flower in the dusk. On their soft
    weighbridge
They balanced the light, on their milkmaid's yoke they
    carried it
Over mahogany mountains,
Till the room was breathing its secret to the ghost of the
    wind in the bay.

That radiant patience made a lake of the stern piano
Where she sang *The Isle of Capri*. Such
Beauty in the frail old voice, so long a river of widowhood
The light went running with through the banks of
    shadow . . .

It caught the little pointed breasts of brass
Nubian goddesses on the mantelpiece. It put in the shade
A mysterious cavern under the table
Where African butterflies, in the pinned tomb of their
    wooden boxes,
Spread their gorgeous wings that reeked of camphor.

In my grandmother's house there existed a borrowed
    shrimping net
And a maiden aunt, your best friend ever.
A peacock feather. An ostrich egg. A time
When the breathing of time was audible in gas mantles,
Conspiratorial and benign.

Peculiar Policemen

Sergeant Brown's Parrot

Many policemen wear upon their shoulders
Cunning little radios. To pass away the time
They talk about the traffic to them, listen to the news,
And it helps them to Keep Down Crime.

But Sergeant Brown, he wears upon his shoulder
A tall green parrot as he's walking up and down
And all the parrot says is 'Who's-a-pretty-boy-then?'
'I am,' says Sergeant Brown.

Sergeant Brown's Parrot and Sir Robert Mark

Sir Robert Mark, Police Commissioner,
Heard of a Sergeant who had dared to position a

Parrot on his shoulder. 'A what?' he said.
'PARROT. TALL. GREEN. ALONGSIDE HIS HEAD.

SMART. WELL-SPOKEN. A BIRD OF BREEDING.
PROCEEDS WHEREVER THE SERGEANT'S
    PROCEEDING.'

The report was delivered at a Working Luncheon.
Sir Robert banged his plate with his silver truncheon.

The plate broke in half. No-one dared to laugh.
'Bring this man in!' he roared to his staff.

The Sergeant was working on a dog theft case,
Sitting at his desk with his parrot in place.

'Come on, Brown!' they yelled. 'Better make it snappy –
Sir Robert Mark wants you and he isn't too happy!'

So off went the Sergeant and the parrot and the rest of
    them,
Arrived where Sir Robert was scoffing with the best of
    them.

Sergeant and parrot strolled into the meeting.
Everyone stopped talking. Everyone stopped eating.

Sir Robert looked the pair of them up and down
With a dangerous look in his eye. He said, 'Brown,

I've seen some things in the Force, my *word* upon it,
But never once a Sergeant with a shoulder with a bird
    upon it.

Take it off at once, you ridiculous clown!'
'Shut your beak,' said Sergeant Brown.

Sergeant Brown's Parrot's Girl-friend

Sergeant Brown's parrot's girl-friend
Squawked to herself in a hickory tree:
'They say my parrot boy's no good,
They say he's lousy as can be.
   They put him down
   In every way
   But what I say
Is: Good enough for Sergeant Brown
   Is good enough for me!'

That splendid Sergeant Brown
That strides about the town!

So Sergeant Brown's parrot's girl-friend
Flew till she came where Sergeant Brown,
Her tall green lover on his shoulder,
Was pacing grandly up and down.
   She whispered low
   In her lover's ear:
   'It's me, my dear.
Tell me, truly, who's-a-pretty-girl-then?'
   'I am,' said Sergeant Brown.

That frightful Sergeant Brown
That strides about the town!

The Great Detective

Oh, I am the greatest detective
　　The criminal world's ever known,
For my eyesight is never defective
　　And my ears are entirely my own.

I've never been stuck for an answer,
　　I've never been troubled by doubt,
Dismay or confusion: I form my conclusion
　　By sorting the evidence out.

Last night I came home. As I entered,
　　I straight away lighted upon
The fact that the telly was off from the way
　　I could see that the thing wasn't on!

I noticed a man in there, *sitting* . . .
　　A man that, I know, sometimes stands.
I could tell by one look he was reading a book
　　From the book that he held in his hands!

I heard a voice call from the landing.
　　It wasn't my sister or brother.
I could tell that the voice was my own mother's
　　　　voice
　　Since the voice was the voice of my mother!

It shouted, 'Get up here and tidy
　　Your bedroom!' The man who sat reading
Made no move at all in response to the call,
　　Neither left foot nor right foot proceeding.

A curious case. I imagined
    Some sort of a misunderstanding.
That the yell came again I knew instantly when
    The yell came again from the landing

Highly suspicious. The evidence
    Seemed to me, nonetheless, thin.
Tiptoeing the floor, I departed once more
    By the very same door I'd come in.

Yes, I am the greatest detective
    The criminal world's ever known,
For my eyesight is never defective
    And my ears are entirely my own.

Monty Makes It

Monty was a Mountie on the plains of Manitoba,
He was very seldom saddled, he was very seldom sober,
And they murmured round the province and across
    Sas-kat-chew-*an*
That Monty was a Mountie
Who *never* got his man.

Woody was a dog-thief working down in old Toronto,
He was hounded, he was hunted, so he left Toronto
    pronto
And he headed for the prairies where grain-elevators rise
For he figured he'd lie *doggo*
Beneath those mammoth skies.

Now Monty gets to snoozing after far too much libation.
Outside the little tavern snores the owner's huge Alsatian
When there comes a gravel growling and a yelping and a
    yowl.
Up awake springs Monty.
'A dog-thief's on the prowl!'

The moment Woody catches that, he thinks he'd best
  skedaddle.
Out the bar reels Monty and he leaps up for the saddle,
But he doesn't just quite make it though he never hits the
  ground.
No, coming down like thunder,
He lands *astride the hound*!

Which takes off like a blizzard through the miles of
  standing wheat
With Monty hanging on by all his elbows, chin and feet,
And the guys inside the tavern, well, they rate his chances
  slim.
'Say goodbye to Monty.
Last we seen of him!'

So what's become of Woody? Well, he's figuring to sneak
Inside a big red barn that stands beside a winding creek,
When he turns and, to his horror, his dismay and
  consternation,
There's Monty coming at him.
He's back – on the Alsatian!

It's looking bad for Woody. What to do now, where to
  hide?
He staggers back, forgetting he's beside the waterside,
Which might not be disastrous nor his prospects quite so
  dim
Except for just one detail:
Woody cannot swim!

Now Monty's had a drink or two, the dog has not had
    one,
So it's dusty, hot and thirsty from the circuit it has run
And it races for the water like a living lightning streak.
Splash! Ker-rash! Ker-rikey!
It jumps into the creek.

So poor old Woody's sinking for the third time out of view.
Monty hauls him out and puts him on the dog's back too
And they flounder from the water and they gallop from
    the shore,
Till, bounding from the wheatfield,
They hit the tavern door!

The charge? Attempted dog-theft, and old Woody has
    confessed.
The guys inside the tavern, they say, 'Monty, we're
    impressed.'
So they murmur round the province and across
    Sas-kat-chew-*an*
That Monty is a Mountie
Who ONE TIME GOT HIS MAN!

Take It Slow

The Catch

You'll receive a
Vauxhall Viva
if you win our
competition:

oh, well done, sir,
you have won, sir,
here's the keys to
the ignition:

off you go now,
take it slow, now,
MIND OUR WALL –
oh dear, a skid, sir:

what a spill, sir,
here's our bill, sir:
you owe *us*
a thousand quid, sir!

Uncle Joe's Jalopy

When you're riding in my Uncle Joe's jalopy,
Better hang on tight cos the roads are pretty choppy
When you're travelling in that car.

It's a dumpy little jumpy little bumpy little number
And it doesn't pay to sleep and it doesn't pay to slumber
And you'd best not go too far
When you're travelling in that car.

It's got holes in the roof the snow has snowed through,
Holes in the floor you can see the road through,
Holes in the dash the petrol's flowed through –
Pretty scary car!

It's got broken springs – brakes on the blink –
Wheels that wobble – fumes that stink –
And the windscreen's turned as black as ink
So you can't see where you are
When you're travelling in that car:
So you'd best not go too far!

But don't you *criticize* that jalopy
Or Uncle Joe will get mighty stroppy
Cos he really likes that car!

When he's at the wheel of that old bone-shaker
He thinks he's a Grand Prix record-breaker –
He thinks he's a motor star!

When he bangs round corners on two square wheels,
Folks on the pavement take to their heels
Cos they don't feel as safe as Uncle Joe feels
When he's travelling in that car:

And as for me, I can't wait for the day
When the wheels fall off and the roof blows away
And Uncle Joe will just have to say,
'Well, that's the end of that car:
It really can't   go too   far!'

Football Fanatics

The Man Who Invented Football

The man who invented football,
He must have been dead clever,
He hadn't even a football shirt
Or any clothes whatever.

The man who invented soccer,
He hadn't even a *ball*
Or boots, but only his horny feet
And a bison's skull, that's all.

The man who invented football,
To whom our hats we doff,
Had only the sun for a yellow card
And death to send him off.

The cave-mouth was the goal-mouth,
The wind was the referee,
When the man who did it did it
In 30,000 BC!

The Rovers

My Dad, he wears a Rovers' scarf,
He wears a Rovers' cap,
And every Saturday before
He goes to see them fail to score,
    He sighs, 'Oh no!
    Why *do* I go?
    They haven't got –
    They've really not –
A rat's chance in a trap!'

    And sure enough
    They always stuff
      The Rovers.

My Dad, he wears a Rovers' tie,
Two huge rosettes as well,
And every time before he leaves
He sits and hangs his head and grieves:
    'I must be mad –
    They're just so **BAD**!
    They haven't got –
    They've really not –
A snowball's hope in hell!'

    And sure enough
    They always stuff
      The Rovers.

Rovers' ribbon, Rovers' rattle,
Dad takes when he's off to battle:
Shouts and stamps and stomps and rants.
DAD'S GOT ROVERS' UNDERPANTS!

Rovers' eyes!
Rovers' nose!
Rovers' elbows!
Off he goes

And sure enough
They always stuff
The Rovers.

EXCEPT
One glorious day,
It didn't work that way . . .
This was the state of play : . .

A goal-less draw,
But just before
The final whistle went,
Rovers stole
The only goal:
I can't say it was *meant*:

What happened was
A wobbling cross
Back-bounced off someone's bum –
And Praise the Lord!
Rovers scored!
They'd won! Their hour had come!

So Dad, he whirled his Rovers' scarf,
  He hurled his cap up high.
'Oh, we're the best there's ever been!
We're magic!' he yelled out. 'You've seen
  Nothing yet.
  Just wait. We're set!
  Yes, you can bet
  The lads will get
Promotion by and by!

Our luck is in –
We're *bound* to win –
  Us Rovers!'

It didn't work that way,
Alas for Dad.
That goal's the only goal
They've ever had.

Now every Saturday before
He goes to see them lose once more,
    He sighs, 'Oh no!
    Why *do* I go?
    They've got a curse –
    They're getting *worse* –
How *can* they be so bad?'

And sure enough
They always
STUFF THE ROVERS!

Out to Lunch

Rock Around the Wok

There's a frying and a frizzling
    and a simmer and a sizzling
    in the WOK . . .

There's a bunch o' crazy beanshoots
    and the shoots are pretty meanshoots
    in the WOK . . .

There's a ginger root a-jumping
    and a lotta stalks a-stumping
    in the WOK . . .

There's onions that are springing
    and there's flavours that are singing
    in the WOK . . .

    So,
    Baby,

    LET'S GO STIR THE WOK
    (Oh, baby)
    LET'S GO STIR THE WOK
    (Oh, baby)
    ROCK AROUND THE WOK

Because:

There's a lotta food,
  There's a lotta heat.
So shake it up!
  That's enough.
  Let's eat

FROM THE WOK!

Give Up Slimming, Mum

My Mum
is short
and plump
and pretty
and I wish
she'd give up
slimming.

So does Dad.

Her cooking's
delicious –
you can't
beat it –
but you really can
hardly bear
to eat it –
the way she sits
with her eyes
brimming,
watching you
polish off
the spuds
and trimmings
while she
has nothing
herself but a small
thin dry
diet biscuit:
that's all.

My Mum
is short
and plump
and pretty
and I wish
she'd give up
slimming.

So does Dad.

She says she
looks as though
someone had
sat on her –
BUT WE LIKE MUM
WITH A BIT
OF FAT ON HER!

Say Cheese

At Christmas the STILTON
Was spilt on the Wilton,
The rare CAMEMBERT
Was as fine as can be,
But at New Year the GRUYERE
It just went straight through yer,
The CHEDDAR was bedder
But as for the BRIE,

Aaaaaaaagh! And the PORT SALUD!
Swallow one morsel, you
Kept to your bed
For a week and a day,
And if you tried WENSLEYDALE
You quite *immensely*'d ail,
Hospital-bound
Till they wheeled you away!

No better was EMMENTHAL,
Sour and inclement, all
Cratered and pocked
Like a view of the moon!
And while some are crazy
For creamed BEL PAESE,
Myself, I'd eat forcemeat
Or horsemeat as soon!

The LEICESTER was best o'
The bunch, but the rest o'
Them curled up your stomach.
Though GLOUCESTER (times two)
And jaundiced old CHESHIRE
I'd taste under pressure,
Nothing would get me,
No, nothing would get me,
But nothing would get me
To try DANISH BLUE!

Greedyguts

I sat in the café and sipped at a Coke.
There sat down beside me a WHOPPING great bloke
Who sighed as he elbowed me into the wall:
'Your trouble, my boy, is your belly's too small!
Your bottom's too thin! Take a lesson from me:
I may not be nice, but I'm GREAT, you'll agree,
And I've lasted a lifetime by playing this hunch:
The bigger the breakfast, the larger the lunch!

The larger the lunch, then the huger the supper.
The deeper the teapot, the vaster the cupper.
The fatter the sausage, the fuller the tea.
The MORE on the table, the BETTER FOR ME!'

His elbows moved in and his elbows moved out,
His belly grew bigger, chins wobbled about,
As forkful by forkful and plate after plate,
He ate and he ate and he ate and he ATE!

I hardly could breathe, I was squashed out of shape,
So under the table I made my escape.

'Aha!' he rejoiced, 'when it's put to the test,
The fellow who's fattest will come off the best!
Remember, my boy, when it comes to the crunch:
The bigger the breakfast, the larger the lunch!

The larger the lunch, then the huger the supper.
The deeper the teapot, the vaster the cupper.
The fatter the sausage, the fuller the tea.
The MORE on the table, the BETTER FOR ME!'

A lady came by who was scrubbing the floor
With a mop and a bucket. To even the score,
I lifted that bucket of water and said,
As I poured the whole lot of it over his head:

'*I've* found all my life, it's a pretty sure bet:
The FULLER the bucket, the WETTER YOU GET!'

Eating Cheaply

You can eat, if you are plucky,
Though you've not 1 p to spend.

Simply order hot fried chucky
For yourself and for your friend,

And complain: 'THIS CHICKEN'S MUCKY!
It's disgusting! It's the end!

It's uneatable! It's yucky!
You can't *seriously* pretend

This is *food*? Why, you'd be lucky
If a *rat* would eat it! Send

The lot back to the chuckery
Where it came from! I intend

To report this matter, ducky:
That means CURTAINS, FINISH, END!'

But

All the time you're knocking it,
Keep wolfing it. Make sure
You've bolted all the chicken down –

THEN

Bolt out through the door!

If You're No Good at Cooking

If you're no good at cooking,
Can't fry or bake,

Here's something you
Can always make. Take

Three very ordinary
Slices of bread:

Stack the second
On the first one's head.

Stack the third
On top of that.

There! Your three slices
Lying pat.

So what have you got?
A BREAD SANDWICH,

That's what!
Why not?

Sprout
(for Laurel and Hardy)

On the long road leading out of Cambridge,
On the trail of the loathsome sprout . . .

When the sun was out,
I tweaked your snout.
You said I was a person
You could do without.

Oh, March,

Where potatoes have the starch,
Not the sprout!

I'm so loathsome to you-hoo!

On the long road leading out of Cambridge,
On the trail of the loathsome sprout!

The Cat's Pyjamas

Pride

Two birds sat in a Big White Bra
    That swung as it hung
    On the washing-line.

They sang: 'Hurray!' and they sang: 'Hurrah!
Of all the birds we're the best by far!
Our hammock swings to the highest star!
    No life like yours and mine!'

They were overheard
    By a third
    Bird

That swooped down on to a nearby tree
And sneered: 'Knickers! It's plain to see
A bird in a tree is worth two in a bra.
    There's no bird *half* so fine!'

And it seemed indeed that he was right
For the washing-line was *far* too tight
And old and frayed. As the laundry flapped,
The big wind heaved and the rope . . . *snapped*!

You should have heard
    The third
    Bird.

He cried: 'Aha!
For all their chatter and la-de-dah,
They didn't get far in their Big White Bra!
If there *is* a bird who's a Superstar,
It's me, it's me, it's me!'

Down to the ground
He dived in his glee

And the Big Black Cat
Enjoyed his tea.

Cleaning Ladies

Belly stuffed with dust and fluff,
    The Hoover moos and drones,
Grazing down on the carpet pasture:
    Cow with electric bones.

Up in the tree of a chair the cat
    Switches off its purr,
Stretches, blinks: a neat pink tongue
    Vacuum-cleans its fur.

Applause

I gave my cat a six-minute standing ovation
For services rendered: hunting of very small game,

Pouncing about and sitting in cardboard boxes,
Three-legged washing and never knowing his name,

The jump on the knee, the nuzzle at night, the kneading
Of dough with his paws, the punch at the candle flame,

The yowling for food, the looking at everything otherwise,
Staring through it straight with a faraway aim.

I gave my cat a six-minute standing ovation.
Your cat's like that? I think you should do the same.

Dad and the Cat and the Tree

This morning a cat got
Stuck in our tree.
Dad said, 'Right, just
Leave it to me.'

The tree was wobbly,
The tree was tall.
Mum said, 'For goodness
Sake don't fall!'

'Fall?' scoffed Dad,
'A climber like me?
Child's play, this is!
You wait and see.'

He got out the ladder
From the garden shed.
It slipped. He landed
In the flower bed.

'Never mind,' said Dad,
Brushing the dirt
Off his hair and his face
And his trousers and his shirt,

'We'll try Plan B. Stand
Out of the way!'
Mum said, 'Don't fall
Again, OK?'

'Fall again?' said Dad.
'Funny joke!'
Then he swung himself up
On a branch. It broke.

Dad landed *wallop*
Back on the deck.
Mum said, 'Stop it,
You'll break your neck!'

'Rubbish!' said Dad.
'Now we'll try Plan C.
Easy as winking
To a climber like me!'

Then he climbed up high
On the garden wall.
Guess what?
He *didn't fall*!

He gave a great leap
And he landed flat
In the crook of the tree-trunk –
Right on the cat!

The cat gave a yell
And sprang to the ground,
Pleased as Punch to be
Safe and sound.

So it's smiling and smirking,
Smug as can be,
But poor old Dad's
Still

Stuck
Up
The
Tree!

Who's a Good Dog?

Bad Dog Blues

Well, I shake my coat when my coat gets wet,
      And the fam'ly call me a pesky pet,
And they chew me out just for chewin' their shoes.
         They call me Bad Dog . . .
            I got the Bad Dog Blues.

You can hear me round the hills and over the crags
      When I'm on one of my barking jags,
And you won't want to listen but you can't refuse
         Cos I'm a Bad Dog . . .
            I got the Bad Dog Blues.

When the folks are lyin' on the beach all day,
      And there's never a one of them wants to play,
I slobber their ears when they're tryin' to snooze,
         Cos I'm a Bad Dog . . .
            I got the Bad Dog Blues.

If there's one thing I like (and I like it all the time)
      It's a dive in the ditch to the deep dark slime.
Then I roll on the rug and I seep that ooze,
         Cos I'm a Bad Dog . . .
            I got the Bad Dog Blues.

Now you're never gonna stop me chasin' a cat,
　　　I guess my brain's just wired like that,
So felines find me pretty Bad News,
　　　　Cos I'm a Bad Dog . . .
　　　　　　I got the Bad Dog Blues.

Well, every little thing ought to have its place,
　　　Like the place for a nose is upon a face.
Maybe dogs like me ought to be in Zoos . . .
　　　　Cos I'm a Bad Dog . . .
　　　　　　I GOT THE BAD DOG BLUES!

Guide-dog Blues

Howling city high road or rutted country track,
If the harness be a-straining, or if the reins be slack,
Dog here, boss, right with you: take you by hell and back.

Dog here, boss, through the winter's slithery slush and
    slime,
Eyes for you in the springtime leafing of beech and lime:
But why do we never seem to want to pee at the same
    time?

Heads or Tails?

Dave Dirt's dog is a horrible hound,
    A hideous sight to see.
When Dave first brought it home from the pound,
We couldn't be certain which way round
    The thing was supposed to be!

Somebody said, 'If that's its *head*,
    It's *far* the ugliest dog in town.'
Somebody said, 'The darned thing's *dead*!'
    'Don't be silly, it's *upside-down*!'
'It's *inside-out*!' 'It's a sort of *plant*!'
'It's wearing *clothes*!' 'It's Dave Dirt's *aunt*!'
    'It's a sort of *dressing-gown*!'

Each expert had his own idea
    Of what it was meant to be
But everybody was far from clear –
    And yet . . . we *did* agree
That Dave Dirt's dog was a horrible hound
    And a hideous sight to see!

It *loves Dave Dirt*. It follows him round
    Through rain and sun and snow.
When set in motion, it looks far *worse*,
And nobody knows if it's in reverse . . .
    Or the way it's supposed to go!

Hot Dog

My Dad can't stand my sister's latest boyfriend.
Boring?

When he comes round, even the dog
Starts snoring.

Our hamster crawls back in beneath
His straw. *Dad grits his teeth.*

Our budgie

Folds his wings and shuts up shop.
Dad's eyelids drop.

Boring?

What he goes on about
Is Being A Vegetarian.
His line is 'Meat is Out'
And his line doesn't vary an
Inch. It goes like this:

GIVE HAMBURGERS A MISS!

EVERYONE IS MISTAKEN
WHO EVER EATS BACON!

THE ENTIRE WORLD SHOULD STOP
FANCYING A PORK CHOP!

He's utterly convinced
Of the evil of beef, minced.

If he were God, he'd damn
All lamb. And ham. And spam.

What's best, he says, for you
Is lentil-and-seaweed stew.

He feels all meals should be:

Lentil-and-seaweed
Stew for breakfast,
Seaweed-and-lentil
Stew for tea.

Oh, he's *sincere* all right:
You couldn't doubt it.

But why must he
Go on and on
And on and *on*
About it?

My Dad can't *stand* my sister's latest boyfriend.
Boring?

Last night I really thought
That Dad would hit him.
What happened was the dog
Woke up and bit him.

My sister was really mad.
They stormed out. Dad

Sat stroking the dog and murmuring
Over and over again,
'Who's a good boy, who's a good boy,

Who's a *good dog*, then?'

Snoozing by the Boozer

All day outside the boozer snores
The boozer-keeper's big brown dog
And carefully each boozer-user
Coming to or from the boozer
Steps around the shaggy snoozer,
     Dumped there like a log.

It chanced a fellow named de Souza
(An American composer)
Once was passing by the boozer
Humming to himself a Blues. A
Dog-enthuser, this de Souza,
So he halted by the boozer.
With his stick he poked the snoozer.
'Big brown dog,' he said, 'say who's a
     Good boy then?' This shows a

Lack of knowledge of the boozer-
Keeper's dog. It is a bruiser,
     Not a dreamy dozer.

Up it sprang and ate de Souza,
The American composer.
He is dead, the dog-enthuser.

Don't poke dogs outside the boozer.
You are bound to be the loser.

A Ballroom for St Bernards

*(In the Craiglands Hotel in Ilkley, Yorkshire,
there is a large space called St Bernard's Ballroom.
Can it be for dancing dogs?)*

Head to head
    And paw to paw,
The big St Bernards
    Tread the floor.

Round and round
    The room they go
In a quickstep that
    Is rather slow . . .

For at huge weights
    They tip the scales,
Lolling their tongues
    And wagging their tails!

Paw to paw
    And snout to snout,
St Bernards all
    Go stepping out,

And each tells each
    As they foot it finely:
'My Great Big Darling,
    You dance *divinely*!'

Excellent People and
Corking Couples

Gary the Great

Watching cricket one June day
When folk in sunlight basked,
I wandered round the boundary
Until I stopped and asked
An old man who'd made many Junes
And many sad Octobers,
'Who was the best you ever saw?'
He said, '*Sir Garfield Sobers*.

'*Sir Gary was the best of all*
Who could both strike and bowl a ball.
In few the twin arts marry,
But since you're looking for a name
That honours most this funny game,
My friend, I give you Gary.

'*He bowled fast-medium or slow,*
He hit six sixes in a row,
That's quite a way to carry:
And every run he ever made
Seemed effortless. The ball obeyed
His bat: I give you Gary.'

I walked away. He called me back.
'Friend, cricket is a *live* scene,
And younger ones will make more tons –
He's just the best one *I've* seen!'

Mercy

Mercy her name was,
The blind lady.
Took her home from bingo
Each Wednesday night,
With her stick tap-rapping
On the breeze-blocks.
She'd humour and love.
No sight.

And suddenly
I recall
Salt of a tide of darkness
Swirling up under that door
She swam through with her key
And turned no light on.
Why should she?
She left all light
Behind her,
Needing none
To find things there:
Things, it seemed,
Could find her.

Mercy.
Took her home from bingo
Each Wednesday night,
With her stick tap-rapping
On the breeze-blocks.
Mercy.
Heart of light.

Our Lady of the Five Ways

Did you ever see Josie dancing
Where five ways meet,
On a wedge of pavement all on her own
Pistoning at the street?

A V of railings shapes her stage
And iron grey are the bars,
Where not-quite-right-in-the-head poor Josie
Dances for the cars.

On and on through the summer night
And traffic roar,
Josie rolls and rocks to a rhythm
You never quite knew before.

For the tune belongs to Josie
And the words are all in her mind.
In her own strange joy and suffering,
Josie makes us kind:

Makes us remember where we are
And the road of love we tread.
Oh, dance on in your dancing heart
For Josie's singing head.

Dallas and Missie

Most of their lives they'd lived in China,
  Came home after the longest while,
Old Mr Ralph and his sister Missie
  With her silver hair and her beautiful smile.

Little Miss Ralph and her brother Dallas
  In his curious hat like a woven pie,
Keeping an even flame of kindness
  On Pilgrims' Way in the days gone by . . .

They took a shine to me and my brother.
  The petrol mower sang up and down
As we cut the grass, then painted their high-wheeled
  Romany caravan cream and brown.

None of this really needed doing
  But we were thrilled to be trusted, paid
Pocket money, and loved it when Missie
  Brought ginger beer or lemonade.

I think they sometimes liked children near them,
  However clumsy with brush or blade,
Thank you, Dallas, and thank you, Missie,
  For all of the happiness you made.

Finbar

flowers of frost
bloom
on the pane
ice
in the arms
of black trees
glints
Finbar
is born
from his mother's
womb
by forceps
plucked
like
winter
fruit

his fingers   reach
to the rising   sun

his heartbeat
warms   the
fro   zen
day

Well Done, George

The poet George MacBeth possessed
The worst handwriting in the West.
It looked like smuts discharged by fire,
Or argumentative barbed wire,
Or bracken trampled in a wood.
You get the point. It wasn't good.

And yet the words he wrote were rare
And splendid and beyond compare.
Lucky for us, he typed them out
So no one had the slightest doubt,
When they were printed in a book,
That they were *really* worth a look!

So if your scrawl's a scrum or splatter,
Nest of nostril hairs, no matter.
Think of George, who couldn't get
The letters of his *name* to set,
And practise WELL DONE, GEORGE because
A nicer man there never was.

Candy and Joe

Candy and Joe lived hand-to-mouth
    And yet saw eye-to-eye.
They were neck-and-neck in their love for each
    other
Till the sweet old by-and-by.

They were hand-in-glove till push came to shove,
And it got to the old no-go:

LADIES AND GENTS,
THEY WERE EXCELLENT PEOPLE,

LET'S HEAR IT
FOR CANDY AND JOE!

The Rotters

From early enough in the morning
Till moon made its mark,
Mr and Mrs Rotter
Sat on a bench in the park.

Side by side, most dearly,
They were their favourite friends,
Candles that lit each other
Down to the candle-ends.

When sky was terracotta,
Baked in the late sun's ray,
Mr and Mrs Rotter
Held hands at the end of the day.

When riverbank sun like an otter
Slid in out of sight,
Mr and Mrs Rotter
Kissed at the birth of night.

The last words that they whispered
Tenderly, stars above?
'My dear, you are a Rotter!'
'And so are you, my love!'

The Jellyfish Reunion

Two old jellyfish

who hadn't seen each other
for *years*

wobbled and hobbled
and hobbled and wobbled
over a lumpety
bumpety beach
to meet for a chat
and a snifter
of seaweed
after all that
time.

What's new with you?
Not much. And you?
Not much with me.

So two old jellyfish

who wouldn't see each other
for *years*

hobbled and wobbled
and wobbled and hobbled
back over the lumpety
bumpety beach

and snuggled
into the sea.

Useful Person

We'd missed the train. Two hours to wait
On Lime Street Station, Liverpool,
With *not a single thing to do*.
The bar was shut and Dad was blue
And Mum was getting in a state
And everybody felt a fool.

Yes, we were very glum indeed.
Myself, I'd nothing new to read,
No sweets to eat, no game to play.
'I'm bored,' I said, and straight away,
Mum said what I knew she'd say:
'Go on, then, read a book, OK?'
'I've *read* them *both*!' 'That's no excuse.'

Dad sat sighing, '*What* a day . . .
This is precious little use.
I wish they'd open up that bar.'
They didn't, though. No way.

And everybody else was sitting
In that waiting-room and knitting,
Staring, scratching, yawning, smoking.
'All right, Dad?' 'You must be joking!
This is precious little use.
It's like a prison. Turn me loose!'

('Big fool, act your age!' Mum hisses.
'Sorry, missus.'
'Worse than him, you are,' said Mum.)

It was grim. It was glum.

And then the Down's syndrome child came up
Funny-faced:
Something in her body wrong,
Something in her mind
Misplaced:
Something in her eyes was strange:
What, or why, I couldn't tell:
But somehow she was beautiful
As well.

Anyway, she took us over!
'Hello, love,' said Dad. She said,
'*There*, sit *there*!' and punched a spot
On the seat. The spot was what,
Almost, Mum was sitting on,
So Dad squeezed up, and head-to-head,
And crushed-up, hip-to-hip, they sat.
'What next, then?' 'Kiss!' 'Oh no, not that!'
Dad said, chuckling. '*Kiss*!'
                                    They did!

I thought my Mum would flip her lid
With laughing. Then the Down's syndrome child
Was filled with pleasure – she went wild,
Running round the tables, telling
Everyone to *kiss* and yelling
Out to everyone to sit
Where she said. They did, too. It

Was sudden happiness because
The Down's syndrome child
Was what she was:
Bossy, happy, full of fun,
And just *determined* everyone
Should have a good time too! We knew
That's what we'd got to do.

Goodness me, she took us over!
All the passengers for Dover,
Wolverhampton, London, Crewe –
Everyone from everywhere
Began to share
Her point of view! The more they squeezed,
And laughed, and fooled about, the more
The Down's syndrome child
Was pleased!

Dad had to kiss another Dad
('Watch it, lad!' '*You* watch it, lad!'
'Stop: you're not my kind of bloke!')
Laugh? I thought that Mum would choke!

And so the time whirled by. The train
Whizzed us home again
And on the way I thought of her:

Precious little use is what
Things had been. Then she came
And things were not
The same!

She was precious, she was little,
She was useful too:
Made us speak when we were dumb,
Made us smile when we were blue,
Cheered us up when we were glum,
Lifted us when we were flat:
Who could be
More use than that?

> Down's syndrome child,
> Funny-faced,
> Something in your body wrong,
> Something in your mind
> Misplaced,
> Something in your eyes, strange:
> What, or why, I cannot tell:
> I thought you were beautiful:
>
> Useful, as well.

A Day at the Races

Edward Woodward went to Goodwood
   Every time he could.
If Edward Woodward could make Goodwood,
   Edward Woodward would,

   Would Woodward.

Once he put a lot of bunce
   Upon a wild grey mare.
Instead of trackward, it went backward,
   Edward didn't care!

   No,

Edward Woodward went to Goodwood
   Every time he could.
If Edward Woodward could make Goodwood,
   Edward Woodward would.

   This

Jolly good actor, then he backed a
   Sorrel running *yet*!
Did Edward quarrel with the sorrel?
   No, he didn't fret!

   Oh,

Edward Woodward went to Goodwood
  Every time he could.
If Edward Woodward could *make Goodwood,*
  Edward Woodward would!

(Would Woodward?)

Arnos Grove

Arnos Grove is a London neighbourhood,
Arnos Grove is a place to go,
Arnos Grove is a kind community,
Oldsters smile there, young ones grow.

Arnos Grove means a different thing to me,
Arnos Grove seems a shortish chap
In a small tweed hat with a feather tucked in it,
All of his friendliness there on tap.

I shall go with the evening Londoners,
Dusk be purple or dusk be mauve,
I shall walk till the end of everything
Down with Arnos through the Grove.

A Simple Story of Accrington Stanley

A nasty old woman once lived in Accrington Town
With a face that was blocked with rage like a stopped
   clock,
And she spoke harsh words in a sort of a strangled voice,
Like a person who for some reason has swallowed a sock.

But mostly she said nothing at all. It was no good
Wishing that woman good morning or calling,
   'Goodnight',
But there was a boy in Accrington Town called Stanley
Who thought to himself he just might put things right.

He was kicking a football about on a waste-ground patch
By ragwort and chickweed against a garage wall,
And he spied a Coke can and widened the V-hole out
With a stone, and cut himself not too badly at all.

Then he stuffed the blazing ragwort and frosty chickweed
And mauvely smouldering willowherb into the can
And ran with it round to the nasty old woman of
   Accrington,
Who sat as lonely as an empty removal van.

Croaked, 'Why have you brought me this?' 'It's a present,'
   said Stanley.
'A present? Not ever has anyone brought me one.'
'Well, I have,' said Stanley. 'And so you have!' cried the
   lady,
And danced both up and down and shone like the sun.

Then she took his hands and jigged with him round the
    kitchen,
One foot up, then one and a half feet down,
And ever since then has been known as the jolliest woman
That ever pranced the streets of Accrington Town!

Well, an aeroplane would be good and an elephant
Is always acceptable, but they're hard to find,
And whatever you've got will do wonderfully well if you
    mean it;
Be kind to someone who's stuck. It makes them kind.

Frankie and Johnny Are Useless

Now, Frankie's a nimble showjumper,
Like Princess Anne over the course,
But she jumped the waterjump one day
And that waterjump drowned her horse –

It was her thing
But she did it wrong.

Well, Johnny's a brilliant goalie,
I've not seen a better one yet,
But he let through so many goals one game,
Bust a hole in the back of the net –

It was his thing
But he did it wrong.

Now, Frankie's a dab hand at cooking,
She was cooking the family treat,
But she cooked it so well you just couldn't tell
The potatoes from the meat –

It was her thing
But she did it wrong.

Well, Johnny's a dazzling skater,
On skates he's as good as they come,
But he fell over so many times one night,
Should have worn skates on his bum –

It was his thing
But he did it wrong.

Now, Frankie is *good* on the cello,
You really should hear Frankie play,
But she played it so badly the audience left
And the cello walked away –

It was her thing
But she did it wrong.

Well, Johnny's a master chess player,
Yes, Johnny's amazing at chess,
But he hit that board so hard with his knee,
Where the pieces were – anyone's guess –

It was his thing
But he did it wrong.

Now, I've written a dim little poem,
I've sung you a boring old song,
Told so many lies, can't believe my eyes,
And I've gone on far too long –

Well, it's my thing
But I've done it wrong!

Farmer Jessop

Old Farmer Jessop is a friend of mine
And he ties up the hay with baling twine . . .

In a knot.
That's what.
Oh he ties up the hay in a knot, that's what,
And everything works out fine.

Old Farmer Jessop is a friend of mine
And he fishes for trout with baling twine . . .

On a hook.
In the brook.
Oh he fishes for trout on a hook, in the brook,
And he ties up the hay in a knot, that's what,
And everything works out fine.

Old Farmer Jessop is a friend of mine
And he holds up his pants with baling twine . . .

They're secure.
That's for sure.
Oh he holds up his pants, they're secure, that's for sure,
And he fishes for trout on a hook, in the brook,
And he ties up the hay in a knot, that's what,
And everything works out fine.

Old Farmer Jessop is a friend of mine
And he flosses his teeth with baling twine . . .

Twice a day.
They're OK.
Oh he flosses his teeth twice a day, they're OK,
And he holds up his pants, they're secure, that's for sure,
And he fishes for trout on a hook, in the brook,
And he ties up the hay in a knot, that's what,
And everything works out fine.

Just fine.

Index of First Lines

Acknowledgements

Macmillan Children's Books would like to thank Puffin Books for permission to reprint the following poems from *Cat Among the Pigeons*, copyright © Kit Wright 1984, 1987:

Zoe's Ear-rings; Nothing Else; Mirror Poem; Sid the Rat; Acorn Haiku; The Magic Box; Zoob; What Was It?; Mr Angelo; Something He Left; Freeze; Mercy; Finbar; A Simple Story of Accrington Stanley; Applause; March Dusk.

*How do prawns
spend an afternoon?*

Find the answer to this and many other questions
in this wonderfully witty collection of verse from
the irreverent Kit Wright!

CAT
AMONG THE
PIGEONS

9780141032367 £4.99

puffin.co.uk

A selected list of titles available from Macmillan Children's Books

The prices shown below are correct at the time of going to press. However, Macmillan Publishers reserves the right to show new retail prices on covers, which may differ from those previously advertised.

The Jumble Book
Poems chosen by Roger Stevens   978-0-330-46865-7   £4.99

Sensational!
Poems chosen by Roger McGough   978-0-330-41344-2   £6.99

The Kingfisher Book of Children's Poetry
Poems chosen by Michael Rosen   978-0-7534-1708-9   £6.99

I Had a Little Cat
Collected Poems for Children by
    Charles Causley   978-0-330-46411-6   £6.99

All Pan Macmillan titles can be ordered from our website, www.panmacmillan.com, or from your local bookshop and are also available by post from:

Bookpost, PO Box 29, Douglas, Isle of Man IM99 1BQ

Credit cards accepted. For details:
Telephone: 01624 677237
Fax: 01624 670923
Email: bookshop@enterprise.net
www.bookpost.co.uk

Free postage and packing in the United Kingdom